Shaka Zulu

Learns to Dance

A Kunda Kids Book

Written by
Louisa Olafuyi &
Oladele Olafuyi

Illustrated by
Isabelle Irabor &
Tiolu Yoloye

This book belongs to:

_____

© 2020 Kunda Kids Ltd
Shaka Zulu Learns to Dance
Written by Louisa Olafuyi & Oladele Olafuyi
Illustrated by Isabelle Irabor & Tiolu Yoloye
Designed by Louisa Olafuyi
Edited by Krystle Appiah

First published 2020 by Kunda Kids Ltd

001

Printed and bound in Great Britain by Ex Why Zed Printers
www.exwhyzed.co.uk

ISBN 978-1-8382795-3-0

Follow Kunda Kids
kundakids.com
@kundakids

Shaka Zulu, a real influencer

Shaka Zulu Learns to Dance is a fictional story based on a real-life king, Shaka Zulu, one of the most influential monarchs of the Zulu Kingdom, part of modern-day South Africa.

Shaka Zulu is remembered for being a strong and courageous leader, often described as a genius and one of Africa's great nation builders.

Kunda Kids
Inspiring The Next Generation

Kunda Kids illuminates incredible people from African history and celebrates their contribution to the world.

The stories we tell are fiction, but the people they're based on existed. Each real-life hero was brave, generous or incredible in their own way. Through our stories, we hope to inspire the next generation of leaders, thinkers and game changers.

Meet Shaka Zulu, a great warrior and powerful king.
The Zulu Empire spread far and wide under him.

The empire was vast and filled with animals big and small. There were so many lions, lizards and buffalos all across the land that Shaka couldn't count them all.

Shaka was strong, strict and brave.
With him in charge, the people always behaved.

Just look at his might.
Just look at his stance.

There was only one problem.
Shaka couldn't dance!

Zulu people are known for their great moves.
They can shimmy, shake and really move to the groove.

The leaders in the nearby kingdoms knew the latest dance moves. Shaka was the only king who couldn't move with the tunes.

At parties he tried to follow along,
but he danced like he couldn't hear the song.

His arms and legs would go all wonky.
Some people joked and said that he danced like a donkey.

All the laughing and pointing made Shaka feel very sad.
He didn't have the dancing skills everyone else seemed
to have.

In two days it would be the Zulu disco,
and as the king of the land, Shaka had to go.

The pressure was on. He needed to find a beat,
any beat that could work with his two left feet!

The next day, on a walk through the town,
the king heard a sound.

Bang, ba-ba-bang bang!

It was very loud.

He followed the noise and found his friend, Sandile, drumming on a drum set with her twin sister, Andile.

They played a **boom, bap, a tap and a tip.**
Shaka did the Gwara Gwara and then he did a flip.

He raised his leg and stomped it down,
then moved his hips round and round.

Sandile said, "My King, I see you like my beats.
It's quite unique how you move your feet."

Shaka felt shy and said, "Don't mind me.
Please ignore my little prance.
Your music is great,
but I know that I can't dance."

Andile said, "Those are the best moves I've seen in a while.
You can be yourself. Everyone has their own style."

"Don't compare yourself to other people.
When the music starts we are all equal."

Shaka walked home feeling confident
that his own style was unique.
Soon he stopped saying that he had two left feet.

The day arrived and the time to party was finally here.
Everyone came together with glee and cheer.

Shaka arrived and took a deep breath,
ready to put his moves to the test.

Usually he would hide, but today he was front and centre, smiling and waving at everyone as he entered.

He did a wiggle, a dip, a kick and bow,
followed by a hop and a spin.
And the crowd said, "Wow!"

Shaka's moves were the same, but now he had confidence
so he enjoyed dancing in front of an audience.

In the end he had so much fun,
and his moves became a signature Zulu dance,
enjoyed by everyone.

Shaka learned that we are all created different
and confidence in yourself
is what makes you magnificent.